A Pal For Martin

Distributed to schools and libraries
in Canada by
SAUNDERS BOOK CO.
Box 308
Collingwood, Ontario, Canada L9Y 3Z7
(800) 461-9120

ISBN 089565-756-2
Library of Congress Cataloging-in-Publication Data
available upon request

A Pal

For

Martin

author: Christiane Renauld
illustrator: Corderoc'h

The Child's World
Mankato, Minnesota

He had Mommy and Daddy, of course, and there were the toys and the books.

But what Martin really needed was a pal. A real live pal, with nothing else to do but listen to him and be his playmate, someone who needed Martin's company as much as Martin needed his. The more he thought about it, the more he wished it could really happen, and the more lonesome he felt.

At six o'clock, when Mommy came home from her job, Martin was still sitting on the floor in the middle of the room.

Mommy came over to him. She stroked his hair. She said,

"Come into the kitchen with me." So Martin went along with Mommy. But he was still sad.

Mommy emptied the grocery basket. Tomatoes, leeks, carrots — nothing very exciting. Lettuce — Martin hates lettuce! But there, in the fold of a leaf, was a shiny little black ball!

"What's that?" asks Martin.

"A slug."

"A slug? Poor little thing!"

"Poor little thing? Gardeners can't stand slugs, you know."

Maybe gardeners can't, but Martin's not a gardener. He has no lettuce to protect, and that poor little slug is all alone, just like he is!

Martin dashes to his room.

"Quick, find a box. Not too big, not too small. Not this one. Not that one either. Ah, here we are..."

Martin hurries back to the kitchen. But...

"My slug! Where's my slug?"

"I threw it out," says Mom.

"My slug!" wails Martin, "My poor slug! My friend!"

He dashes to the garbage can. How can he get into that dark hole? How would he ever be able to find a slug in there? Especially a black slug!

"Look," said Mommy, in a very sad voice, "Surely you weren't thinking of raising a slug? A snail, OK, maybe. But a slug??

The following Sunday, Daddy, Mommy and Martin got
into the car. They drove a long way out into the
countryside. They walked in the rain for a long time.

In the evening, there were terrible traffic jams on the freeway. Everyone was dirty and tired.

But Martin went to sleep happy. For on his night table, in a pretty blue box lined with lettuce, there is a snail. His very own snail.

Every afternoon when he comes home from school, Martin has tons of things to tell his snail. Sometimes Snail turns a deaf ear. He stays curled up in the bottom of his shell. Then Martin shakes him a bit, or taps very gently on the shell with the tip of his finger nail, as if at the door of a little house.

"Say, are you there! Are you listening?"

Even homework time is fun now. Martin sets his friend
on the desk and lets him come and go while he is doing
his work. He scatters obstacles in his path: a pencil, a
ruler, an eraser. Snail patiently goes around them or
slowly climbs over them. And Martin cheers him on with
all his might.

"Come on! Come on!"

Now and then Martin asks him for a bit of help.

"What is 7 plus 4?"

Snail never utters a word, but as soon as Martin asks the question, the answer pops into his head.

Life has been wonderful since Snail has been around. Martin has even started to like lettuce!

Then one evening it began to rain. Martin had the idea of putting Snail out on the balcony. "Go on, old fellow, make the most of it!" And that is exactly what he did...

When Martin went to get the snail at dinner time, there was nobody there.

They looked everywhere — explored every flowerpot, every plant, every leaf. Nothing. Not the slightest sign of him. The rain had washed every trace away.

Then Martin had an idea. He took a large sheet of
cardboard, and in his best handwriting, he wrote:

Notice

A snail of the common gray breed has strayed from the 6th floor balcony. If found, please return to Martin, his friend.

He put up the notice in full view by the elevator door and
went back upstairs to his apartment with a heavy heart.

That evening Martin refused to eat any lettuce at all.

The days went by.

Gradually Martin's hopes began to fade. Then he gave up hoping altogether. He told himself that snails were never meant to live in boxes, not even pretty blue ones lined with fresh leaves. Anyway, he still had Mommy and Daddy and the toys and the books.

What he did not know yet was that Daddy and Mommy were preparing a wonderful surprise for him.

Just a few months later, there was Martin striding home
from school with his bag on this back. He didn't stop by
the toyshop window, nor even at the candy store. He was
hurrying home to be with a round,

pink little creature that lived at his house now. A real
live Someone, who had nothing to do except listen to
him, and who would soon be able to be a playmate for
him. Someone who needed Martin as much as Martin
needed him.

His little brother.

THE CHILD'S WORLD LIBRARY

THE LOVE AFFAIR OF MR. DING AND MRS. DONG

LULU AND THE ARTIST

THE MAGIC SHOES

THE NEXT BALCONY DOWN

OLD MR. BENNET'S CARROTS

THE RANGER SMOKES TOO MUCH

RIVER AT RISK

SCATTERBRAIN SAM

THE TALE OF THE KITE

TIM TIDIES UP

TOMORROW WILL BE A NICE DAY

THE TREE POACHERS